Rapscallion Jones

JAMES MARSHALL

The Viking Press, New York

For Ronald Kolodzie

First Edition
Copyright © 1983 by James Marshall
All rights reserved
First published in 1983 by The Viking Press
40 West 23rd Street, New York, New York 10010
Published simultaneously in Canada by Penguin Books Canada Limited
Printed in U.S.A.
1 2 3 4 5 87 86 85 84 83

Library of Congress Cataloging in Publication Data
Marshall, James, date.   Rapscallion Jones.
Summary: A debonair fox, finding himself past his
prime and short of funds, decides it is not too late
for him to make his fortune as a writer.
[1. Foxes—Fiction. 2. Authorship—Fiction] I. Title.
PZ7.M35672Rap 1983   [E]   83-4817
ISBN 0-670-58965-9

In the middle of a cold and wet afternoon,
in a dingy boardinghouse on the other side of town,
Mr. Rapscallion Jones was just beginning to stir.
"No need to get up quite yet," he said.
"I have no pressing engagements."
But as Rapscallion pulled up the covers,
someone knocked at the door.

It was Mama Jo, who ran the boardinghouse.

"Now see here, Jones," she said. "Your rent is long overdue, and I'm tired of waiting!"

Rapscallion explained that he was presently short of funds.

"Then get a job!" said Mama Jo.

Rapscallion couldn't believe his ears.

"But I am a *fox*!" he said. "Foxes don't *work*!"
"Never too late to reform," said Mama Jo.
"Get a job or else!"
Rapscallion had to sit down.
What was the world coming to?

"Maybe I could marry a rich widow," he said.

Brushing his yellowing teeth in rusty tap water,
Rapscallion studied himself in the mirror.

"My, my," he said. "I've certainly let things slide.
Clearly I'm no longer in my prime.
But perhaps the old pizzazz is still there."

He tried to look interesting and debonair.
"Hello, ladies," he said to the mirror.

But there was no doubt about it—
the old pizzazz *was* gone.
"I shall have to try something else," he said.

At dinner Rapscallion made a startling announcement.
"I have decided to become a writer," he said.
"Ha!" said Mama Jo. "You call *that* a job?"

The other boarders were impressed.
"That's hard work," they said.
"Not for those with talent," said Rapscallion.

That night Rapscallion began his new job.

He used up six tablets of paper, two bottles of ink,

and a whole box of paper clips.

He drank cup after cup of strong tea.

But by morning every sheet of paper had the same words

written on it: Once upon a time…

Once upon a time…

Once upon a time…

"I seem to have hit a snag," said Rapscallion.

He decided to get some air.

"How's the writing coming?" asked a boarder.

Rapscallion pretended not to hear.

Outside it was very unpleasant—wet and cold.
In a nearby park Rapscallion saw some young ne'er-do-wells
lolling about in the rain and talking ugly.
"Look at that guy in the funny clothes," they said.

"I," said Rapscallion, "am a writer."
"You are not," said the ne'er-do-wells.
Rapscallion showed them his inky paws.

"Then tell us a story," they said.
"With pleasure," said Rapscallion.
"Once upon a time…once upon a time…hmmm…"
Just then two crocodiles crossed the park.

Rapscallion was reminded of something from his youth.
"I've got it!" he said. "Lend an ear, lads, while
I tell you a tale about the clever Rapscallion Jones…"

Once upon a time a debonair young fox
in the prime of his life, set out to take the country air
and to stir up some mischief.
Soon he came upon something that caught his interest—
a spiffy roadster parked by the road.
"Hmm," said the fox, "I think I'll go for a spin."

So he jumped into the driver's seat,
started up the engine,
and tore off down the road.
Somewhere in the next county
he noticed a small black bag on the seat beside him.
"I wonder what's in there," he said.

At that moment he heard a frantic call.
"Doctor, doctor, is that you?" cried a lady.
The fox stopped the roadster.

"Yes, it is I," he said.
"Come quickly!" said the lady.
"My poor husband is getting worse!"

In a small upstairs bedroom
a large crocodile lay suffering and groaning.
His stomach was horribly swollen.

The fox noticed right away that the floor
was strewn with little crumpled-up balls of silver foil.
Clearly, the crocodile had been eating chocolate kisses!

"I have overindulged," said the crocodile.
"Will you give me some little pink pills?"
The fox had an idea.
He took the crocodile's pulse.

And he looked very serious.
"This is the worst case of chocolate poisoning
I have ever seen!" he cried.
"Say your prayers, croc!"

The crocodile's wife screamed.

The patient's pulse grew faster.
"Isn't there anything that can be done?" he said.
The fox scratched his chin.
"I'll think of something," he said.
"But my fees are high."

"Oh, don't worry about money," said the lady.
"We have *scads* of it."
"Really?" said the fox.
The lady lowered her voice.

"We put it in the refrigerator
to keep it nice and crisp," she said.
"In that case, I will help," said the fox.

"But you must follow my instructions exactly.
It is important to redistribute the chocolate
in the patient's system."
"Yes, of course," said the crocs. "That makes sense."

"You must jump up and down on the bed
with all your might," said the fox.
"And don't stop until I tell you."

The crocs began the treatment right away.
They were so grateful to the kind doctor.
But while they were bouncing up and down
(and occasionally bumping into the ceiling),
the fox crept downstairs to the kitchen.
In the refrigerator he found a bag
full of dollar bills—all nice and crisp.
He took it all,
and off he went!

"And *that*," said Rapscallion Jones, "is how one clever fox outsmarted *two* crocodiles."

"Hot dog!" cried the ne'er-do-wells.
"That's the best story we've ever heard!"
And they decided then and there
to be just like that clever fox when they grew up.

They begged for another story.
But Rapscallion had to get home to his writing.
He left the park feeling pleased.
"Well, well," he said, "I seem to have a story."

But sitting in the rain had given him a chill,
and when he got home, he took to his bed.

That night the situation went from bad to worse.
A doctor was summoned.
"There is nothing I can do for this fox," he said.

"He's a goner," said Mama Jo.
"And he never paid his rent."

At midnight a minister was called.
"Is there anything you want to tell me?" he said.
"Yes," said Rapscallion in a weak voice,

"that story I told the lads in the park..."
"Yes?" said the minister, leaning closer.

"I didn't tell the whole truth," said Rapscallion.
"I wasn't such a clever fox after all.
The crocodiles' money was only play money."
"Poor thing," said Mama Jo. "He's gone off his head."
"Not telling the truth can make you ill," said the minister.

"Crime does not pay," said Rapscallion.

And he fell back into the pillows.
He closed his eyes.
"There's nothing more I can do," said the minister.
Mama Jo and the other boarders sat by the patient's bed
all through the night.

The following day, sometime after sunrise

Mr. Rapscallion Jones made a startling recovery.
"Well, look who's here," said the other boarders.
"I'm giving up this writing business," Rapscallion said.
"It's bad for my health."

"And what about the rent?" said Mama Jo.

"Yeah," said the boarders.

"Don't worry about that," said Rapscallion.

"I have something in mind."

"This better be good, Jones," said Mama Jo.

THE WONDERFUL FEAST

By Esphyr Slobodkina

 GREENWILLOW BOOKS, New York

Early in the morning
Farmer Jones got up.
He stretched himself
and said,

"It is, indeed,
a beautiful morning.
The sun is shining bright,

the corn has grown tall,
the birds are singing fine,
and I feel fine too!"

Then he went into the shed
and gave his horse a great
big measure of feed.

"My," said the
old horse, Spotty.
"What a wonderful
feast I'm going
to have!"

He ate all he wanted
and went to sleep.

**Then
everything
was quiet
again,**

and

nothing was heard but the sleepy sighs of Spotty.

While
Spotty slept,
little she-goat
Nanny wandered
into the shed.

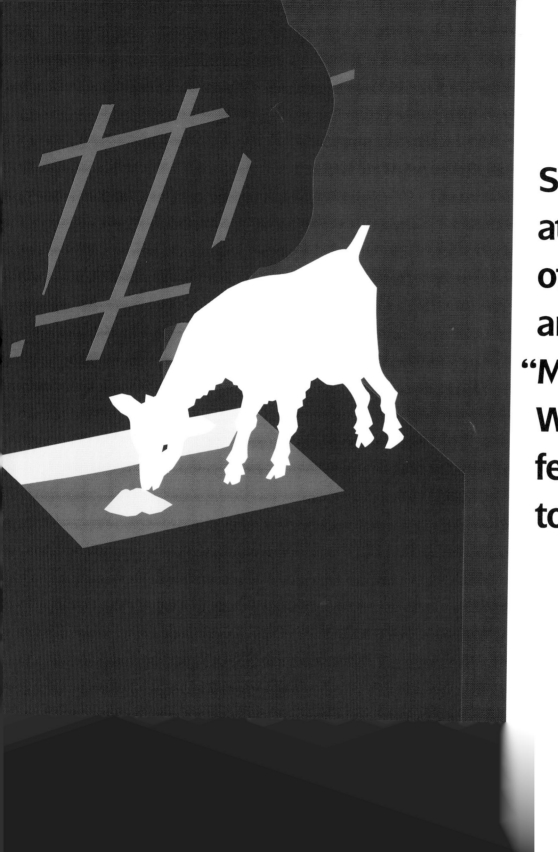

She looked
at what was left
of Spotty's meal
and said,
"My, oh, my!
What a wonderful
feast I'm going
to have!"

She ate all she wanted and
wandered out of the shed.

Just then

the red hen,
Strawberry, walked in,
looking for her breakfast.
"Children, children," she called.
"Look what a wonderful
feast we are going
to have!"

In a moment the floor was covered with little yellow chicks, and there was a great noise and commotion while they had their meal.

But all was quiet again in the shed after they left.

"Oh, my—
oh, my—
oh, my!"

whispered a little mouse,
peeping out of his hole.
"What a wonderful feast
I'm going to have!"

He quickly crossed the
floor where the few scattered grains lay
and took all he could to his house.

And then a busy
old ant crawled in,
searching for
winter supplies.

He picked up the last grain
and carried it away,
muttering all the time to himself,

**"My, oh, my!
What a wonderful feast I'm going to have!"**

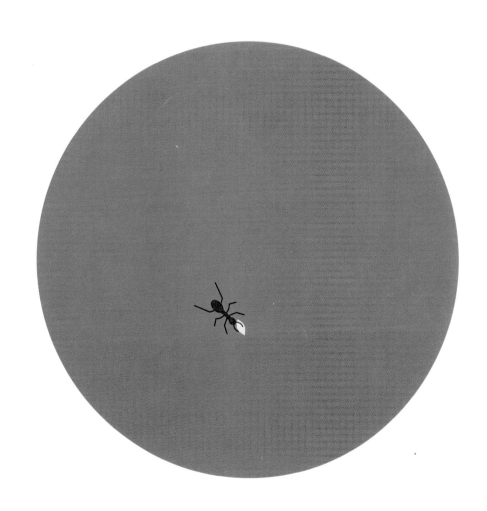

Library of Congress Cataloging-in-Publication Data
Slobodkina, Esphyr (date)
The Wonderful Feast / by Esphyr Slobodkina.—
New, rev. ed.
   p.   cm.
Summary: Farmer Jones feeds his horse
a wonderful feast, and from what is left
a number of other animals also have
a wonderful feast.
ISBN 0-688-12348-1.
ISBN 0-688-12349-X (lib. bdg.)
[1. Domestic animals—Fiction.]
I. Title.
[PZ7.S6334Wo   1993]
[E]—dc20
92-23416   CIP   AC